D0463150

GREAT TALES FROM LONG AGO

ODYSSEUS AND THE ENCHANTERS

Retold by Catherine Storr
Illustrated by Mike Codd

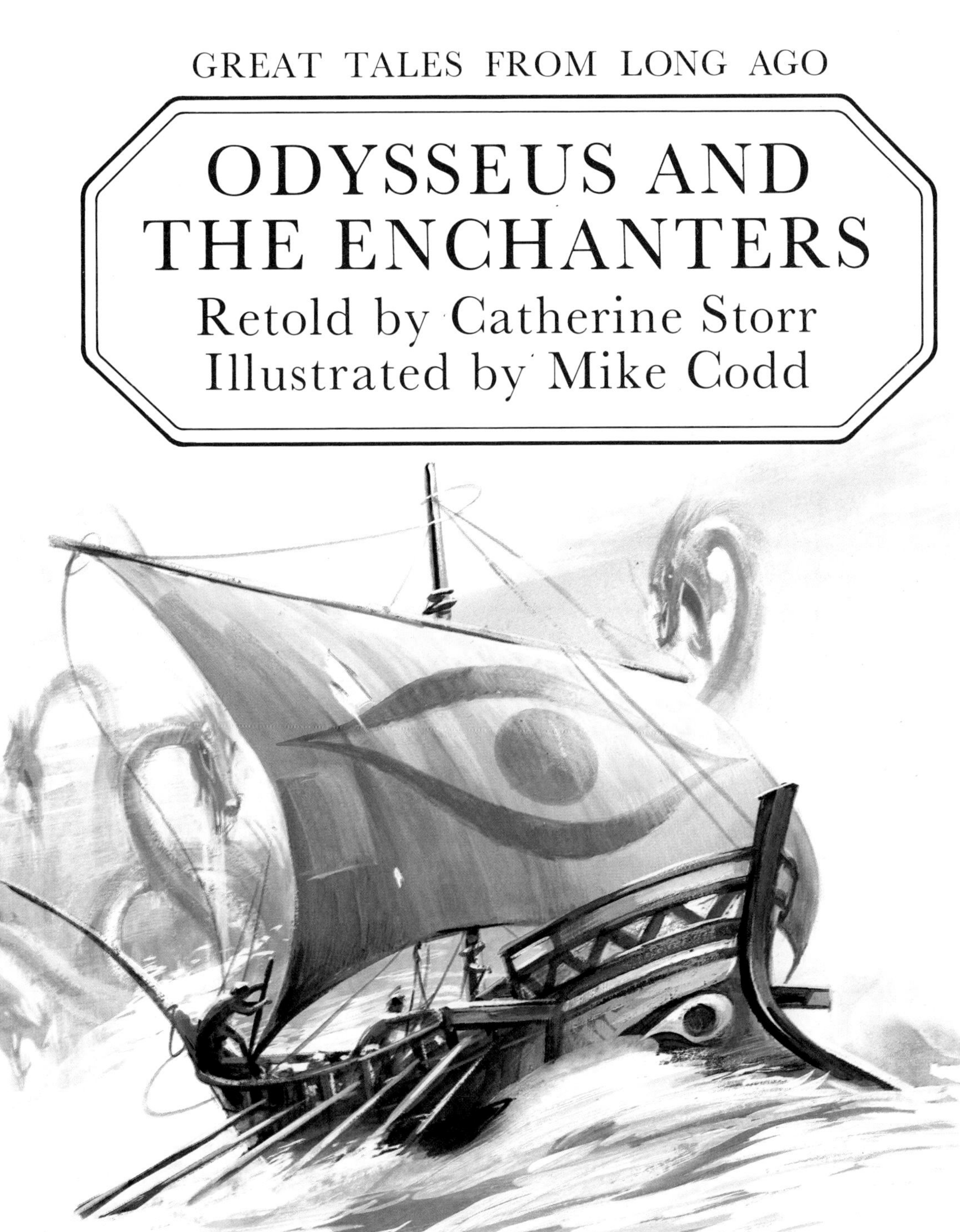

Methuen Children's Books
in association with Belitha Press Ltd.

Art Director: Treld Bicknell
First published in Great Britain in 1985
by Methuen Children's Books Ltd,
11 New Fetter Lane, London EC4P 4EE
Conceived, designed and produced by Belitha Press Ltd,
2 Beresford Terrace, London N5 2DH
ISBN 0 416 53570 4 (hardback)
ISBN 0 416 54000 7 (paperback)

Printed by Purnell & Son (Book Production) Ltd,
Paulton, England

FAR AWAY IN THE SEAS AROUND GREECE,
lay a small island covered with thick forests.
Men told strange tales about it.
"Sailors who land there are never seen again,"
said one old man.
"Nonsense! My son was there once
and he saw lions and wolves roaming the woods.
They looked wild, but when they saw my son
they stood on their hind legs like men,"
said another man.

ODYSSEUS, THE CLEVEREST OF THE GREEK HEROES,
was sailing back after the Trojan war
to rocky Ithaca, his kingdom.
When he reached the mysterious island,
he was exhausted, after escaping great dangers.

FOR TWO DAYS, HE LAY ON THE BEACH,
getting back his strength.
On the third day,
Odysseus took his spear and his sword
and climbed the cliffs to see what the island was like.

He reached the top of a hill
from which he could see the whole island.
From among the thickly planted trees,
he saw a wisp of smoke rising into the clear air.
He went back to the shore,
carrying meat for his hungry companions,
and that night they ate and drank and were refreshed.

THE NEXT MORNING,
Odysseus divided the ship's company
into two parties of twenty-two men in each.
They cast lots, and it fell to Eurylochus,
one of the officers, to take his party of men
to explore the island.
Odysseus and the others stayed on the shore.

Eurylochus and his men climbed the hill
and they, too, saw the smoke
rising from among the trees.
As they approached, they saw a beautiful palace
in a clearing of the forest.
From the open windows of the palace
came the sound of someone singing a sweet song.
They were astonished to see the palace surrounded
by mountain wolves and lions,
who came towards them, wagging their tails
and trying to caress them.
The sailors ran for safety towards the palace.
The doors opened, and a beautiful woman
stood there and invited them to come in.

Almost all the men followed her into the palace.
Eurylochus was the only one who stayed outside,
fearing that this might be a trap.
He looked through a window, and saw Circe, the witch-goddess,
give the men a sweet drink, mixed with a drug
which made them forget their country, their wives, their children.
Then she touched them with her wand,
and drove them to the pigsties.
For each one had become a pig,
with pigs' bristles and a pig's snout.
They could not speak, they could only grunt.

Eurylochus was horrified.
He rushed back to the shore to tell Odysseus.
Odysseus took his sword and his bow
and set off alone towards Circe's palace.

AS HE WENT, HE SAW A BEAUTIFUL YOUNG MAN IN HIS PATH.
The young man took his hand, and said,
"Odysseus, do not look for your companions here.
Circe, the witch-goddess,
has penned them into her sties, like swine.
She will do the same for you
if you do not do exactly what I tell you.
I am going to give you something
that will keep you safe from Circe's magic.
When she tries to turn you, too, into a pig,
draw your sword and threaten to kill her.
Make her promise to release your companions
and not to try any more of her tricks."
The young man bent down and picked a little plant.
Its petals were milk-white and its root was black.
He said, "This herb is called Moly,
and it will protect you.
It is difficult for men to dig up,
but we gods can do anything."
Then Odysseus knew that this was no ordinary man,
but Hermes, the messenger of the gods.

AS ODYSSEUS APPROACHED CIRCE'S PALACE
he heard the witch-goddess, singing at her loom.
He called out, and Circe came to the door
and welcomed him, as she had his companions.
She led him in, and gave him a rich drink
in a golden bowl.
Then she touched him with her wand, and said,
"Go and join your friends in the sty."
But the herb, Moly, protected Odysseus,
and he remained in his own shape, as a man.
He drew his sword as if he meant to kill Circe.

Circe fell to her knees. "Who are you?" she cried.
"Do not kill me! Stay here in my palace,
and trust me, and learn to love me!"
But Odysseus remembered the warning of Hermes.
He made Circe promise to turn his friends back into men,
and to play no more tricks.
Then her maids bathed Odysseus in warm water,
and clothed him in a fresh tunic and cloak.
They set before him and Circe
fine food on silver plates
and sweet wine in golden goblets.

ODYSSEUS TURNED AWAY.
"I cannot eat nor drink
while my companions are still spell-bound," he said.
Then Circe went to the sties
and drove out the herd of pigs.
She smeared each beast with a magic balm
and as she did this, their bristles fell off,
the pigs' snouts disappeared,
and Odysseus saw his dear companions once more.
He wept for joy. Then Circe said,
"Odysseus, go down to the shore
and drag your ship high on the beach.
Then bring the rest of your ship's company back here
and stay with me for a while."

Odysseus did as Circe had asked.
Then he and all the ship's company
remained in Circe's palace for many months,
feasting and singing, and living in soft delight.

At the end of a year, when they were leaving,
Circe warned Odysseus
of the dangers that still lay ahead.
She told him of the Sirens
whose song lured men to death.
She told him of the horrible monsters,
Scylla and Charybdis, and how to escape from them.

ODYSSEUS SAID GOODBYE TO CIRCE
and he and his companions left her island in the ship.
When they were nearing the island of the Sirens,
Odysseus did as Circe had advised him.
He knew that if his sailors heard the Sirens' song
they would sail towards the island
and every man would be lost.
He softened a ball of wax, and with this
he plugged the ears of every man but himself.
He had told Eurylochus to bind him with ropes to the mast,
and not to loosen the ropes, however much he pleaded.

As the ship came near the island,
the Sirens sang an entrancing song.
The sailors could not hear it,
but Odysseus heard it and was filled with longing
to go nearer, to land on the island
and to taste the pleasures promised in the song.
He pleaded with Eurylochus to untie the ropes,
he ordered and he threatened.
But Eurylochus only tightened his bonds
and would not set him free
until they were beyond the reach of the Sirens' song.

NOW THE SHIP CAME INTO THE NARROW CHANNEL
that lay between Scylla and Charybdis.
The men could already see the spray and churning water
and hear the roar of the whirlpool, Charybdis,
as she sucked the water down under the rocks on her side.
On the other side they saw Scylla,
a monster with six heads, grinning teeth,
and twelve grasping feet
which she dangled out of her cave,
high on the rocks opposite Charybdis.

"Row as quickly as you can,"
Odysseus cried to the oarsmen.
"Steer straight on, but keep nearer to Scylla,
for if the whirlpool catches us,
we shall all be lost," he said to the helmsman.
So the ship sped on, swift as a bird,
between the two dangers.
But they were not quick enough.
With her cruel feet,
Scylla snatched up six of the sailors
and crammed them into her six long-fanged mouths.
Odysseus and the others wept for pity and fear,
but now the ship was through the channel
and out on the open sea.

SO ODYSSEUS CONTINUED HIS JOURNEY
knowing he must face many more dangers.
For Poseidon, the god of the sea,
had sworn that it should take him
ten years before he could reach rocky Ithaca.